]

Women's Torah for Our Time

A Festschrift in Honor of
Rabbi Elyse Goldstein

Edited by Rabbi Dayle A. Friedman

Toronto, Ontario

2024

Front cover artwork: Rabbi Geela Rayzel Raphael, see pg. 3
Back cover artwork: Rabbi Tzvia Jasper, see pg. 29

ⒶⓁⒺⓅⒽ
technology

Design & typeset by Baruch Sienna
www.alephtechnology.com

Table of Contents

'Or Ḥadash — Women's Torah Brings New Light

Commentary on Cover Art

Rabbi Geela Rayzel Raphael

T HE MOON pictured on the cover represents the Shekhinah, the Divine Feminine. A woman of fire — the element of spiritual transformation — rides this moon. A colorful tallit and kippah adorn her. Hovering over Jerusalem, holy home of three religions, she represents Judaism, which has been enriched by many new contributions by women in the past half-century.

A Torah scroll is released from the woman's outstretched hand. The Hebrew letters on the scroll spell out the word b'reishit, "in the beginning." Through women's original voices and fresh insights, a new light of Torah, *'or ḥadash*, is revealed. We thus fulfill the biblical wish, *ḥadesh yameinu k'kedem*, renew our days as of old.

A midrash states that the Torah was written with the black fire of the Hebrew letters on white fire. Here a sparkling Hebrew letter aleph, floats in space. It is a mysterious symbol of potential and beginnings — of the unknown, the uncharted. The aleph summons us to ask, what new Torah will tomorrow's feminist perspectives reveal?

Rabbi Dr. Elyse Goldstein

A brief biography

Rabbi Dr. Elyse Goldstein is the founding Rabbi and now Rabbi Emerita of City Shul, a Reform congregation in downtown Toronto she started in 2011, which has grown to prominence as one of the most creative synagogues in Canada. She broke the "stained glass ceiling" right after her ordination upon her arrival to Toronto in 1983 as the only female Rabbi in all of Canada. She was quickly recognized as a fiery speaker, skilled teacher, and social justice advocate. After serving as Assistant Rabbi at Canada's largest synagogue of 5,000 families, Holy Blossom Temple, she moved to Boston to lead Temple Beth David of the South Shore, which she transformed from a small congregation into a thriving community of over two hundred families. She returned to Canada in 1991 to found Kolel: The Adult Centre for Liberal Jewish Learning, an institute recognized as a leader in Jewish adult education; she was awarded the most prestigious prize in Jewish education, the internationally recognized Covenant Award for Exceptional Jewish Educators, in 2005.

Her first book, *ReVisions: Seeing Torah through a Feminist Lens*, won the Canadian National Jewish Book Awards in the field of Bible. Her second and third books, *The Women's Torah Commentary*, and *The Women's Haftarah Commentary* were the first Bible commentaries in history written by female Rabbis. Her fourth book, *New Jewish Feminism: Probing the Past, Forging the Future* won finalist in The National Jewish Book Awards.

Rabbi Goldstein acted from 2017–2019 in "The Clergy Project," an award-winning theatrical production she co-wrote with a priest and a minister, about being clergy in the 21st century. This touching and funny piece won Best of The Fringe Theatre Festival in Toronto. In 2009 she helped found Adat Israel, the only Reform congregation in Guatemala, and volunteered as their rabbi until 2023.

She graduated Summa Cum Laude and Phi Beta Kappa from Brandeis University in 1978, earning her Masters' Degree and ordination from Hebrew Union College-Jewish Institute of Religion. She received a Doctor of Divinity, honoris causis from HUC-JIR 2008. In 2017 she was awarded Doctor of Laws Honoris Causis from Ryerson University, (now known as Toronto Metropolitan University) in recognition of her groundbreaking work in Canada.

Foreword: An Appreciation of Rabbi Elyse Goldstein

Rebeca Orantes

RABBI ELYSE GOLDSTEIN has worked closely with my Guatemalan Jewish family for more than a decade. Throughout those years I have had the privilege of watching her rabbinic professionalism up close, as she displayed skill, passion, strength but, most importantly, deep love for Jewish education. The following words are an attempt to articulate how miraculous her presence has been in our lives, as best-selling author Marianne Williamson says: "A miracle is a shift in perception from fear to love — from a belief in what is not real, to faith in that which is. That shift in perception changes everything." That's exactly what Rabbi Goldstein achieves everywhere she goes; every person she has touched — including us — has gotten to know hope and the self-empowerment that comes with it, a total shift in perception.

Rabbi Goldstein powerfully embodied Jewish ethics when she heard my parents' story and decided to help them build the Reform Jewish congregation in Guatemala, Adat Israel. My mother, Jeannette, and my father, Alvaro, remember fondly the first time they met Rabbi Goldstein, and they still talk about that day as a miraculous encounter. My parents, like many Jewish leaders with great vision for the future, were struggling to see beyond the challenging circumstances that arise when one tries to create something bigger than oneself. Rabbi Goldstein's response was not only empathetic and encouraging but was also the personification of the Divine's response to my parent's prayers.

And as a future rabbi, I ask myself — isn't this something we strive to achieve as religious educators and leaders? After all, not only do we engage in deep study about our tradition and culture in order to transmit their teachings from generation to generation, but we must also be able to connect with people's most profound hopes and encourage them to achieve their dreams from a place of genuine care. The outcome will be a leadership that positively transforms those who are led. Rabbi Goldstein has been my personal example of this principle.

As a woman, I am truly grateful for having grown up with the image of a strong, intelligent, capable, and passionate female rabbi. In Guatemala, the Jewish community comprises less than one thousand individuals. Guatemala is a society where traditional gender roles dominate life.

But because of Rabbi Goldstein's example, I never felt inadequate or insecure about my role within Judaism, my congregation, or the rabbinate; I was too busy admiring her and learning from her to even care about what my society and other streams of Judaism said about women. I am sure I am not the only one who has felt capable of achieving any goal because of her mentorship and encouragement. Doubt never crossed my mind, and as I look back, I conclude that was because I knew it was possible, thanks to her presence in my life.

Beyond inspiring me, Rabbi Goldstein has provided significant support and guidance to our congregation, Adat Israel. She has sought to empower and inspire our local leaders in order to guarantee the future of the community; I was lucky to be one of those who learned from her.

Thanks to the encouragement and fundraising from Rabbi Goldstein, my mother and I were able to travel to the 2017 URJ Biennial in Boston. On this trip, we got to study a variety of topics such as social justice, Jewish sacred texts, and history with top Jewish educators. This trip was transformative for both my mother and me, for it was the first time we found ourselves surrounded by many Jews. I remember dancing, singing and davening next to the two most influential women in my life, while also feeling amazed and delighted by the extraordinary Shabbat and Havdalah services offered at the convention.

Nevertheless, there came a moment at the end of Havdalah when I was overwhelmed by the realization that the rabbinate was imminent in my life. Even though I didn't question my capabilities as a Jewish woman to lead, I did worry about my future: how could a Jewish Guatemalan woman become a rabbi? Deep within me I wondered: "Can I be like Rabbi Goldstein, is that possible?" Tears began running down my face as we sang Debbie Friedman's Havdalah melody, hugging each other while saying goodbye to the Sabbath. Rabbi Goldstein saw me, held my face with both her hands and, seeing the fear in my eyes, she said: "I know it will be hard, but it is possible. You are meant to become a rabbi; we will make it happen. You can do it."

Here I am, seven years later, a third-year Rabbinical student, writing a foreword for this wonderful book that celebrates the rabbinate of Rabbi Elyse Goldstein. This and many more things would not have been possible if it were not for her, and her guidance. Rabbi Elyse Goldstein's impact extends far beyond the borders of Guatemala, transcending cultural and geographical boundaries to touch the lives of countless individuals with her light. She is a source of inspiration for those fortunate enough to know her. Our lives have been full of miracles because she helped us shift our perception of life, and this allowed hope and self-empowerment to radically change us.

Adat Israel thanks you. I thank you.

Introduction: Renewing Our Days

Rabbi Dayle Friedman

הֲשִׁיבֵנוּ יְהוָה אֵלֶיךָ וְנָשׁוּבָה חַדֵּשׁ יָמֵינוּ כְּקֶדֶם
Turn us to You and we shall return; renew our days as of old.
(Lamentations 5:21)

These words from Lamentations, which are part of our Torah service and High Holy Day liturgy, bear an inherent tension. "We shall return." On the one hand, the text expresses a wish to return to the past, to resume a life which has been interrupted by destruction and exile. "Renew our days as of old." On the other hand, we find here a desire for something new and fresh to be brought to our lives. The prayer is not to return to the way things were, but perhaps, to recover the liveliness and passion that we once had. This tension between looking back and looking forward, between tradition and innovation, is deeply embedded in Jewish life and learning.

In her thinking, teaching and writings, Rabbi Elyse Goldstein has masterfully held this paradox; she has, like Isaac, excavated anew the wells of her forbearers, bringing forth a connection to the riches of Jewish heritage. She has leveled fierce critique against the sexism of Jewish life and text, while at the same time remaining deeply rooted in and passionate about the tradition. For example, while rejecting the devaluing of women's bodies of traditions laws of family purity, Elyse was one of the earliest feminists to envision Mikveh as a powerful space for contemporary women.

Rabbi Goldstein has inspired countless Jews through rigorous and brilliant teaching of text at the institute she founded, Kolel: The Adult Centre for Liberal Jewish Learning, and through her visionary leadership of congregations in Toronto, Ontario, Canton, Massachusetts, and Guatemala City, Guatemala. She has renewed the tradition through the fresh perspective of the feminist lens and through her distinctive insight and passion, as is evident in her groundbreaking book, Re-visions: *Seeing Torah Through a Feminist Lens*, and in her creating a platform for other women's creativity in *The Women's Torah Commentary* and *The Women's Haftarah Commentary*. Seeing a need for a vibrant Reform presence in downtown Toronto, she founded City Shul, a congregation that reflects her commitment to serious Judaism, innovation, and gracious inclusivity. Rabbi Goldstein has led City Shul toward remarkable fruitfulness, including the creation of *Siddur Shirat Halev*, which features beautiful artwork, rich supplementary readings, and a gender-inclusive text, and the commission of a sefer Torah written by six women scribes.

It is customary in the academic world to honor an esteemed scholar with the publication of a festschrift, a collection of writings by colleagues and students. As she retires from City Shul and embarks on her next adventures, more than a minyan of women rabbis and thinkers have honored Rabbi Elyse Goldstein by creating this festschrift. Specifically, the authors were invited to contribute a piece of new Torah in tribute to Rabbi Goldstein's Torah. The contributors to this festschrift come from five countries on three continents. They include theologians and chaplains, congregational rabbis, and ritual innovators. They represent the very earliest pioneering women in the rabbinate in North America and Israel, courageous pathfinders in mid-career, and the next generation of spiritual leaders in Judaism. In this book, the contributors have crafted innovative interpretations of biblical texts, personal reflections on Hebrew words and letters, novel approaches to prayers and holidays, and fresh ways of seeing the body and the stages of life. Truly, their radiant words and images represent women's Torah for our time.

A personal note: it is my privilege to serve as editor of this volume. It has been a joy to work with my thoughtful and incisive colleagues, and to watch their Torah take shape. More than this, though, it is my great blessing to count Elyse as my beloved friend of fifty years. We met as camp counselors, and then again as fellow college first-year students. We have shared dorm rooms, apartments, and hotel rooms; we have accompanied each other through life's greatest joys and deepest sorrows. And, perhaps most precious of all, we have been hevruta partners, sharing weekly Torah study across the miles, first on the telephone, then on Skype, and now Zoom. We have studied midrash, chasidut, and Torah commentary from a wide array of perspectives. We once read a Talmudic text that said: the Torah is medicine.[1] The Torah we have explored together has brought us healing in moments of despair, excitement in times of ennui, and always, always given us profound insight into ourselves and our world.

I am ever enriched by my *haverah*, Rabbi Elyse Goldstein. I pray that this collection will truly be an honor to her amazing career, and that she, and all who read it, will find stimulation and inspiration in it.

---

1. Babylonian Talmud, Bava Batra 16a

The Lessons of Tamar, the Person and the Tree

Rabbi Naamah Kelman

Tamar is the name of two women in the Bible, as well as the name of a tree. What associations do we have with the person or the tree? *Tzadik ka·Tamar Yifraḥ*...May the righteous flourish like the palm tree, *tamar* (Psalm 92:13). The *tamar* is a source of abundance. It is rooted in the ground, often indicating a spring of water in the wilderness. Its branches provide shade, and also serve as the lulav; its fruit are the delicious dates; its trunk provides wood for building, for fire. As explained in Genesis Rabbah 41a:

מַה תְּמָרָה זוֹ אֵין בָּהּ פְּסֹלֶת, אֶלָּא תְּמָרֶיהָ לַאֲכִילָה, וְלוּלָבֶיהָ לְהַלֵּל, חֲרָיוֹת לְסִכּוּךְ, סִיבִים לַחֲבָלִים, סַנְסַנִּים לִכְבָרָה, שִׁפְעַת קוֹרוֹת לְהַקְרוֹת בָּהֶם אֶת הַבַּיִת, כָּךְ הֵם יִשְׂרָאֵל אֵין בָּהֶם פְּסֹלֶת, אֶלָּא מֵהֶם בַּעֲלֵי מִקְרָא, מֵהֶם בַּעֲלֵי מִשְׁנָה, מֵהֶם בַּעֲלֵי תַּלְמוּד, מֵהֶם בַּעֲלֵי הַגָּדָה. (בראשית רבה מא, א)

Just as the date-palm has no waste, rather her fruits are for eating, her hearts (*lulavim*) for praise (*hallel*), its branches for s'chach, its fiber for ropes, its boughs for measure, its rafts as beams for the house, likewise there is no waste in Israel, some are masters of Scriptures (Torah), others of Mishnah, others of Talmud, others of Aggadah (narrative tales).

The *righteous*, like the Tamar, shall also stand as sources of sustenance and resilience. What could be more refreshing than a spring in the wilderness, offering shade and fruit? What could be more sustaining and renewing than the ongoing interpretation of Torah?

These qualities are reflected in the first woman named Tamar in the Bible. This Tamar, the twice widowed daughter-in-law of Judah, has waited for a child and a future that Judah has denied her. Only when Tamar disguises herself and seduces Judah will she secure a future for herself as part of his lineage. At first Judah is furious of the news of Tamar's pregnancy, demanding she be burnt to death. But once Tamar proves to Judah that he is the father, a startling occurrence happens; Judah apologizes—*tzadkah mimeni!*—she is more *righteous* than I! (Genesis 38:26)

Tamar teaches Judah the meaning of responsibility, of a commitment to the future and how to repair tragic circumstances. Judah is changed and in charge. Later, when Jacob's sons seek food in Egypt, forced to plead with a Joseph they do not recognize, Judah will be challenged in a different way.

Joseph, now the Viceroy of Egypt, has ascertained that his beloved brother Benjamin has remained in the Land of Israel. Joseph demands that Shimon remain with him as a hostage, only to be redeemed if his brothers bring Benjamin to him. The brothers have no choice but to return to Jacob and plead that Benjamin return with them in order to win Shimon's release. They are scared, guilt-ridden, and hungry as the famine rages. They know that Jacob has kept Benjamin back because of the trauma of losing Joseph. Reuven, the eldest and ever the hot-headed son, offers to kill his own two sons to redeem Shimon if Benjamin doesn't return. But Judah (Yehudah), now steady and mature, knows that will not convince Jacob (who is called Israel throughout their exchange in vss 1-8). Only hope, promise, faith in the future will convince Israel. Judah utters one of the most beautiful sentences in our Torah, in alliterative Hebrew: Judah's name contains the letters of God's name; so when he speaks to Israel, it is not clear who is talking to whom.

וַיֹּאמֶר יְהוּדָה אֶל־יִשְׂרָאֵל אָבִיו שִׁלְחָה הַנַּעַר אִתִּי וְנָקוּמָה וְנֵלֵכָה וְנִחְיֶה וְלֹא נָמוּת גַּם־אֲנַחְנוּ גַם־אַתָּה גַם־טַפֵּנוּ:

Judah spoke to Israel, his father, send the boy with me and we will rise, and walk, and live and not die (***nakuma, nelecha, nichyah, ve'lo namuut***), all of us, and you and our children!

Tamar has taught him and us what it means to take full responsibility as a leader, one who sees far beyond the immediate crisis and one who will take us forward: to live and not die! Tamar has chosen life. We as a Jewish people chose life again and again. Tamar's offspring will be the ancestors of King David, descendants of Ruth, the harbingers of redemption.

And even farther in the future, we meet Deborah, the judge, in the Land of Israel, sitting under a Palm tree (*etz tomer*), meting out *righteous* rulings for the children of Israel. She is no longer disguised, with full autonomy. Unlike Tamar, Deborah is fully visible in her power, embodying her full agency, and able to wield it on behalf of the people.

In these post-October 7th, 2023 days of woe and war, we might draw strength from Tamar, determined to build a future and "speak (and act) truth to power!"

And may we also learn from our namesake, Judah/*Yehudah*, who showed the Jewish people (*yehudim*) the courage to change, to lead and bring the ultimate reconciliation between brothers.

I Dreamed a Dream

Rabbi Devorah Lynn

WHEN I STUDY Torah, I am always on the lookout for what professional scholars call an inclusio. I call them Torah parentheses. An inclusio is a literary device that brackets narrative, prophetic, or poetic text with a word, phrase, theme, or event that opens the parentheses and then is repeated down the line to close the thought, story, or chapter. I'm fascinated by these biblical instances of inclusio because at this time in my life, I notice brackets around periods of my life story that repeat or close a theme started in my youth.

I resonate deeply with an inclusio in the Book of Genesis. This set of brackets, in neighboring portions *Vayetze* and *Vayishlaḥ,* concerns Jacob's abrupt departure from and return to Canaan. This round-trip journey is framed by two dreams, one on his way from home to Haran, and the second on his return to Canaan.

When Jacob flees home to avoid Esau's wrath at his stealing the birthright, he carries nothing with him but a staff. En route to his uncle's home in Haran, he finds himself at dusk at a special place originally called *Luz*. *Luz* is Aramaic for almond and according to the sages, it also refers to either the bone at the top of the cervical spine or the coccyx, the bottom of the spine, "which, say our Sages, never decays and from which a (hu)man's body will be rebuilt at the time of *t'ḥiyat ha·metim* (the resurrection of the dead)." [1]

It is at this remarkable place that Jacob dreams of a ladder resting on Earth and reaching up to Heaven with angels ascending and descending on its rungs. Upon awakening Jacob famously proclaims, "God was in this place and I did not know it." (Genesis 28:16) Awestruck, he further exclaims, "What a place this is, it is nothing but the House of God and the gate to Heaven."

מַה־נּוֹרָא הַמָּקוֹם הַזֶּה אֵין זֶה כִּי אִם־בֵּית אֱלֹהִים וְזֶה שַׁעַר הַשָּׁמָיִם:

Immediately, Jacob takes action. He negotiates a contract with God, sets and anoints a stone pillar, and changes the place name from *Luz* to *Beit El*, House of God.

Jacob begins the first phase of his adult life in Haran, driven by "affluenza," focused on the material side of life. He acquires flocks, wives, in-laws, children, riches, and property. He learns about relationships, husbandry, husbanding, and duplicity. In this first chapter of his adulthood, he fills his life with possessions with all their complications, heartaches, setbacks,

---

1. Kaf Ha-ḥayim 300:1-2; Vayikra Rabba 18:1. Sefaria Source sheet Peninei Halakhah. 7:7:2 https://www.sefaria.org/ Peninei_Halakhah%2C_Shabbat.7.7.2? ven=Peninei_Halakhah,_English_ed._Yeshivat_Har_Bracha&lang= bi

and successes, setting aside the disaster he has left behind in Canaan.

Two decades later, he leaves Haran and heads back towards home, Canaan, with all he possesses. As his estranged twin brother Esau approaches with a large army, Jacob sends his family and his possessions across the River Jabbok. He is exhausted, empty, alone again, having with him only his staff. Once again, he dreams a dream, but this second one is unlike the peaceful first. (Genesis 32:5) During this "dark night of the soul," Jacob wrestles a stranger, later identified as an angel, and confronts his regrets, doubts, and failures. Midrash theorizes that the angel could represent his brother Esau, or even his mother, his father, his wives, or sons, or any and all the shadows that have plagued his life through young adulthood. The dawn brings the end of the attack and Jacob is left with an injury to his hip. I have certainly been awakened after a tumultuous night's sleep with a sore hip or stiff neck. This all-night wrestling is more dramatically physical than the first, more ethereal dream.

This time Jacob is changed both physically and spiritually as he begins a second phase of his long life. His name is transformed from Yaakov, the heel, with its double meaning, to Yisrael, the one who wrestled with the Divine and prevailed. The next day Esau and Yisrael meet in *teshuvah*, forgiveness, and both proclaim they have all they need. Yisrael is clearly grateful. He tells his brother, "God has been good to me, I have plenty,"

(Genesis 33:11). Crediting God and not himself, relieved at
feeling safe, Yisrael wants nothing but to renew his days settled
(*Vayeshev*, the next *parashah*) in a tranquil peaceful place,
Shechem. This is the end of the inclusio. Close parentheses.

But.... Not so fast.

אֵלֶּה תֹּלְדוֹת יַעֲקֹב יוֹסֵף בֶּן־שְׁבַע־עֶשְׂרֵה שָׁנָה הָיָה רֹעֶה אֶת־אֶחָיו בַּצֹּאן

Genesis 37:2 tells us "This is the legacy of Jacob, Joseph was a
seventeen year-old shepherd..." Rashi and Midrash Rabbah
84:5 observe that the trope of this verse places no comma after
"Jacob." This leads these commentators to read verse 37:2 as:
"This is the legacy of Jacob-Joseph..." Rashi rephrases verse 2 as
"the problems of Joseph jumped upon Jacob."

As much as the wrestling made him confront his shadow side
and anxieties, Jacob has not mastered them and there will be
more to come. With twelve sons and only one daughter, we
know his future holds plenty of *tzuris* (trouble).

But Jacob can still dream. Is it any wonder that he loves his son
Joseph, the one who inherits the dreamer trait, more than the
others?[2]

I can imagine father and son discussing their dreams with each
other while pasturing the flocks. Who else in the family would
understand Jacob so well? Though it is not reported in the

---

2. Bereshit Rabbah 84:6 provides an extensive list of commonalities
between Jacob and his son Joseph.

Torah, I imagine that Jacob fitfully dreamed of the resurrection of his beloved son, Joseph, after he is reported dead by the ten brothers who sold him into slavery. Perhaps the first dream of the ladder was a portent of the emotional and tragic ups and downs that would follow Jacob his entire life. The narrative concludes in a surprising way that Jacob could never have envisioned in a dream: Joseph, his beloved son becomes the right hand of the Pharaoh of Egypt.

Coda: When I was eight years old, I dreamed I someday would become a religious leader but what kind I didn't know, as this was well before Sally Priesand became the first woman ordained as a rabbi in North America. That was until I saw Rabbi Elyse Goldstein from a front row seat at Temple Beth David in Canton, Massachusetts and I began to dream I, too, could be a rabbi.

Follow Nachshon's Lead!

Rabbi Rebecca Dubowe

Y EAR AFTER YEAR, we gather around the Passover table to retell the miraculous story of the Exodus. There is a wonderful discussion in the Talmud inquiring as to what might have happened when the Israelites quickly left to escape and then encountered this very big sea. How were they going to cross over? Did God really work alone when the sea split?

The traditional text states that God said to Moses: "Lift up your hands and the sea will split." (Exodus 14:16). Moses held his arms out over the sea and God drove back the sea with a mighty wind for the entire night. The water split. The children of Israel walked in the midst of the sea on dry ground, the waters forming a wall on both sides.

The rabbis of the Talmud explained that God did not work alone, but rather with a person by the name of Nachshon. The rabbis wanted to emphasize that human beings also can create miracles in partnership with others and with God. Nachshon had the ability to lead during a moment of uncertainty, not knowing how the people would cross this very big sea. The rabbis truly believed that, like God, human beings have the ability to hold power, and most importantly, can have the courage to encounter life in such challenging situations.

This is how the rabbis expanded on the story of Nachshon: The Israelites gathered at the water's edge, and Moses lifted his hands as God commanded... and nothing happened. Then, out of the crowd walked a solitary figure: Nachshon, the son of Aminadav, stepped into the water. His family looked on with horror and amazement. They cried: "What are you doing? Where are you going?" Nachshon walked forward like a person possessed – up to his knees, his waist, his chest. The second the water came up just over his nostrils, when he was fully submerged, at that moment and not a second before, the sea split. And the people were able to walk behind Nachshon to liberation, to a place of singing and joy. (Mekhilta Beshallach 6).

According to the rabbis, any human being can be courageous. However, one person's understanding of courage may be different from others. We are created *B'tzelem Elohim* — in God's image. Each one of us is unique and therefore any of us can be courageous. If that is true, then Nachshon could have been anyone, including those who have a disability.

Approximately twenty percent of the greater Jewish community have a disability, including me. Like Nachshon, my friends and I are courageous and let ourselves walk into the great sea, enabling others to follow us to the other side. Yet others may not want to follow us or pay attention to us due to ignorance and lack of awareness.

Thirteen years ago, the Conservative Movement's Committee on Jewish Law and Standards unanimously accepted a teshuvah (rabbinic ruling) that conferred equal status to Deaf Jews in virtually every area of Jewish practice such as: observing the commandments, counting in a minyan, and worshiping using Sign Language. However, at one point in their deliberations, the committee left the question of reading Torah in Sign Language unresolved as they could not agree on whether Sign Language is considered a reading or a translation. Eventually, one witness stood up and, through his interpreter, made this plea: "What I and the Deaf community want is to have the same rights and opportunities as the hearing community. We want to be able to access the word of God the only way we can. Please," he said, his passion and pain clear, "let us have Torah, too. That's all we ask."

What a simple request this person made. Let us have Torah too — that is all we ask. While he may not have used his voice, his request was loud and clear, and thus the rabbis approved of the teshuvah that using Sign Language was a valid approach to reading Torah. This was a significant step to remove not only physical but attitude barriers so that inclusion and full access with a life of Torah is possible.

This person is Nachshon because he took the first step. Others stood behind him not knowing what was possible, and yet they were ready to follow him. My fellow friends with disabilities are risk takers and not always by choice. There is still much to dismantle among those who believe they know what is best for us. The reactions, observations and comments from others can be exhausting, especially for simple things such as when a sign language interpreter, a wheelchair, a cane, a seeing eye dog or even the way one walks into a room.

People cannot imagine what it would be like not to hear the birds sing, nor see the different colors of the rainbow, nor be able to climb a mountain. As a result, there is often a sense of urgency for people to overcompensate to try to fix what one with a disability may lack. People thought Nachshon was mad for going so deep into the water, but he knew what he was capable of doing and perhaps he had a little bit more faith while others did not.

In reflecting on this story, Rabbi Adam Greenwald writes, "Because they [Nachshon and his followers] were brave, there was space for us to walk behind."[1] Who is "us"? I believe that "us" is all of my friends with disabilities and this is where our story really begins. Nachshon's bravery was not stopped by others, instead they followed him, People with disabilities are fully capable of leading and marching towards Sinai as they seek to embrace the accessible sacred Torah together as one inclusive community.

---

1. Rabbi Adam Greenwald. "Children of Nachshon: Liberation Comes Only to the Courageous." https://www.myjewishlearning.com/article/children-of-nachshon/

A Final Word

This essay is in honor of Rabbi Elyse Goldstein and her dedicated commitment and love to the greater Jewish Deaf community. Early in her rabbinic career, she made a tremendous impact on those in the New York Jewish Deaf community who were seeking an inclusive ASL-speaking sacred space. *Kol HaKavod* to my friend and thank you for leading and inviting others to follow Nachshon's lead!

In the Light of Our Mothers

Rabbi Tzvia Jasper

The text of Ruth and Naomi inspired the piece of art that appears on the back cover. This story includes the famous line, "But Ruth replied, 'Do not urge me to leave you, to turn back and not follow you. For wherever you go, I will go; wherever you lodge, I will lodge; your people shall be my people, and your God my God.' " When thinking about this passage, my mind drifts to the women who came before me, the pioneering women rabbis who walked into the unknown. They did not know what the future of their rabbinates would look like, but they trusted in one another, and together, they made their way through the wilderness.

In our text, Ruth and Naomi transform from separate individuals into one entity: a family. In this piece of art, I have used abstract lines to represent that very transformation. It is not clear where one woman starts or stops. Through their bond, they are quite literally interwoven with one another. Furthermore, I believe that Ruth and Naomi had a relationship of trust, respect, and faith. The women in my art represent that by leaning on one another.

One of these figures holds the Torah, adorned with the words, *l'dor vador*, from generation to generation. We are only now reaching the moment when younger female rabbis can turn to older colleagues, finally able to receive from rabbis who look like them. Just like Ruth and Naomi, the younger cohort of female-identifying rabbis are turning to their foremothers to say, where you went, I will go, your Torah will be my Torah, and I will follow you. Together, hand in hand, we walk into the unknown, shielded by the words of our tradition, and our trust in one another.

On Standing Straight: Embodying the Letter *Vav*

Rabbi Tina Grimberg

Dedicated to my mother, Svetlana Grimberg, *z"l*
on International Women's Day

I T IS SUNDAY and I am in the upstairs, sunlit room of our synagogue. This space is dedicated to our children. Around me are first grade students. We are learning the Hebrew alphabet. I am inspired by my students' imagination and spirit. They are also easily bored. To keep their attention, I turn to an experiential technique.

"Choose your favorite letter of the Hebrew alphabet and let's shape it with our bodies," I call out. Within moments, some students drop to the floor and begin to arrange themselves while laughing and pushing each other, others make shapes standing up.

Two girls choose to become the letter *aleph* — one stretches on the floor facing the ceiling and her friend curls up next to her. Another boy chooses to lie on his side while extending his arm and leg forming the letter *gimel*, the first letter of his Hebrew name. A slim, short-haired girl named Naomi stands up, folds her arms along her body, seals her legs together and remains motionless. "What letter are you?" I ask. "I am the letter *Vav*" she says softly.

There is something about this that feels strangely familiar. For a moment I find myself floating out of this classroom into the world of my memories, one I have not explored for a long time.

Three large panel mirrors, one in front and two on each side, reflect my skinny body and multiply it many times. I am no more than eight years old. My mother has brought me for an assessment to the Children's Institute of Kiev, Ukraine that deals with scoliosis and other bone deformities. Despite my aptitude for dance, flexibility and coordination, my posture worries my mother. I often hear her say to me, "straighten your back." It is said to be impossible to be seen by the head of this institute, but my resourceful mother will not give up. Upon finding out that the chief doctor is her old classmate, Mama insists that her daughter be seen only by him.

I am asked to strip down to my white undies and face the mirror. In the mirror, the blue sky and white spring cloud provide a backdrop for my pale face and my poor posture. The doctor exchanges warm pleasantries and even a brief memory of their time in high school with my mother. He examines me. He has a kind face, but I am terribly uncomfortable. With his finger he draws the line along my spine and adjusts my shoulders. The doctor's hands are steady and cool.

"You have time to address this. It will demand work from both of you," he declares.

I look around the room and hope only not to be left to live in this place as other severely deformed children are. On the wooden floor to my right rests a pile of white plaster cast shells in the shape of upper bodies. These shells are used to help children form and reform their postures. These white casts speak of the terrible treatment that will wait for me if I do not do what I am prescribed.

I agree with everything: I promise to do my special, strenuous exercises under the gaze of my mother. I am willing to sleep on a thin mattress over a plywood board. I will engage my stomach muscles many times a day to hold my posture and my chin – and not get annoyed when my mother reminds me to straighten my back, again and again!

Two shallow rivers leave my eyes as I cry from the cold and embarrassment. Before leaving the doctor smiles at my mother and winks at me. "You can still dance..." His white coat disappears in the long hallway of the Institute.

I get dressed.

My mother, energetic, determined and fearless, has saved her daughter. She whispers to my grandmother while stirring the soup: "If her back is crooked and her posture is deformed, how will she build her life? For a girl," she proclaims, placing the lid decisively over the pot, "it is everything!"

Back in the classroom, I smile at Naomi. "You know," I whisper. "Like you, I am also a letter *vav*. Naomi's eyes widen, but by now she is tired of standing straight and motionless. She drops on the floor to chat with her friends. These students are loud and joyful. In time, I will teach Naomi all the secrets and meanings of this slender, modest letter she and I both love.

I will teach her that *vav* is a letter that is very dear to our Jewish story. It is a straight line that reminds us of a spine of the *lulav* branch. A spine of the Jewish people, who despite our challenging history learned to stand upright and lift our chin.

Vav also means a hook in Hebrew. A hook that connects, mystics say, the upper and the lower worlds and us people to each other.

Vav is a dancer with a perfect posture. There is not a dancer in history who does not adjust their posture.

Vav means "and." There is no story or caring conversation that does not include "and."

"And" allows us to develop a thought and to be heard. "And" gives us an opportunity to build a new history that includes new possibilities and endings. "And," the letter *vav,* moves our nuanced thoughts forward. We grow because of many "ands."

Vav represents the numerical value of six; human beings were created on the sixth day.

Vav is a time traveler. In biblical Hebrew, it is a grammatical marvel that can convert the past into the future and our future into the past.

My mother is dead now for nearly ten years and I am a grown woman and a rabbi. I am in Toronto, Canada, standing in front of the mirror in my dance class on Bloor Street. My teacher adjusts my posture, lifts my head, and reminds me to engage my core. All the other students follow. I feel my mother's presence and miss her more than ever.

Vav is a precious commodity. It can be gifted or borrowed, like the *vav* that is missing five times in the name of Eliyahu (Elijah) in the Tanakh. However, it is found in the name of Jacob/ Yaakov, five times, (*Yud-Ain-Kuf-Vav-Vet,*) where it is superfluous and could have been spelled (*Yud-Ayin-Kuf-Vet.*) Our sages tell us that Yaakov borrowed the letter *vav* from Eliyahu and will give it back to Eliyahu upon his return to herald the redemption of Yaakov's children.[1]

Not now, but sometime in the future my student Naomi, will also learn that the past, present and future are connected by the modest letter *vav*. When "and" is present, conversations with those we love continue way past their end, straight into our daily lives and even into our future.

---

1. Yaakov's/Jacob's name spelled with the letter "Vav": Lev: 26:42, Jeremiah (30:18, 33:26, 46:27, 51:19) Eliyahu's name spelled without "Vav": II Kings 1:3, 1:4, 1:8, 1:12 and Malachi 3:23.

Hineni: Here I Am

Rabbi Sally J. Priesand

Hineni (Here I am) is the time-honored response of the Jewish people, the word most often used in the Hebrew Bible by those of our ancestors called by God to be fully present at a time of challenge, ready to respond for the benefit of others and the well-being of all. *Hineni* (here I am): the Jewish response that reflects a great deal about the character, commitment, and integrity of the one who speaks it.

Over the years, I have become accustomed to looking beyond the most basic meaning of Hebrew words by giving each letter a meaning of its own. For example, the word *hineni* begins with the letter *hei,* which in could be seen to stand for the word *hodaah* (gratitude). In Judaism, every day is Thanksgiving. We begin each day with the prayer *Modah Ani*, thanking God for returning our soul and bringing us back to life after a night of sleep. In the *Amidah,* we recite *Modim Anaḥnu Lakh,* expressing gratitude for the many blessings that brighten our days, especially the ones we so often take for granted. Our sages taught that the essence of all prayer should be gratitude, not petition. In other words, we should always approach the act of prayer with grateful hearts, giving thanks for what we have, instead of lamenting the difficulties that come our way.

At times when our patience is mightily tried, we should especially try to look for *Sheheḥeyanu* moments. The *Sheheḥeyanu* is our blessing of gratitude, thanking God for keeping us alive, sustaining us, and allowing us to reach the present moment. It expresses gratitude not only for times and seasons, but also for what we have, who we are, and what life brings our way. If we look for *Sheheḥeyanu* features ingrained in our daily activities and express our gratitude for what we can do, for what we have accomplished, and for what we may yet become, then our lives will truly be touched by the presence of God, and we will be able to face the challenges that come our way with tranquil minds and hopeful hearts.

At the center of the word *hineni,* we find the letter *nun* twice. For our purposes, let this stand for *na·aseh v'nishma* (we shall do and we shall hearken), the words spoken by our people as they stood at Sinai prepared to enter into covenant with God (Exodus 24:7). *Na·aseh v'nishma* reminds us that Judaism requires action; the survival of the Jewish people depends upon each of us, on how we act and what we do. One of our most important responsibilities as members of the Jewish people is turning the words *na·aseh v'nishma* into action, making certain to infuse Judaism into everything we do. This is how we have survived from generation to generation, by striving always to be better Jews and teaching our children and grandchildren to do the same.

The final letter of the word *hineni* is the letter *yud,* which stands for God, a reminder that we are partners with God in completing the world, that our Jewish obligations come from God. Sometimes we fail to notice the difference between the English word *life* and the Hebrew word *ḥayim.* There is an *if* at the center of the word *life*, an *if* that affects the way every person lives. What if Eve had not chosen knowledge over life in the Garden of Eden? What if Pharaoh's daughter had not adopted Moses? What if Miriam and the women had not brought their timbrels to rejoice on the shores of the Sea? What if Deborah had not accepted the mantle of leadership? What if women had never become rabbis? That little word *if* affects the future in ways we cannot even imagine.

The Hebrew word for life is also a four-letter word, *ḥayim,* but unlike its English counterpart, it has in the middle, not that little word *if,* but two *yuds,* which spell the name of God, *Adonai.* If we put God in the center of our lives, and help others do the same, then we can meet any challenge without being defeated or overwhelmed, and we can live with the certainty that life has meaning and purpose and that God depends on us, even as we depend on God.

Hineni (here I am) is the Jewish response when God calls. We congratulate Rabbi Elyse Goldstein as she celebrates her retirement. We are grateful for the lives she has touched, the souls she has taught, and the many contributions she has made to the survival of the Jewish people.

The Holiness of the Body

Rabbi Judith Edelman-Green

W E WHO HAVE devoted our lives to breaking barriers to women's Torah scholarship too often live in our minds and not in our bodies. I have had the blessing of studying the Torah's teachings about body parts with Rabbi Elyse Goldstein. I find these texts offer us both a relationship to the Divine in our bodies, as well as an awareness of our abilities and finitude.

Breasts

As Elyse taught from an article from Rabbi Arthur Waskow, "If we look back at the blessings in which *Shaddai* is over and over invoked, they are about fruitfulness and fertility. God is seen as Infinite Mother, pouring forth blessings from the Breasts Above and the Womb Below. From the heavens that pour forth nourishing rain, from the ocean deeps that birth new life."[1]

We can both physically and metaphorically hug our hurting friends, family, congregations to our breasts. We female Rabbis can teach and exemplify our rabbinate in a unique way; we can exemplify a "hug to our metaphoric breasts." As it is stated in

---

1. Arthur Waskow. "The Breasted God," a Torah teaching for Va-y'chi. The Shalom Center, January, 2007

Isaiah, "As a shepherd(ess) shepherds their flock and gathers lambs to their Divine bosom..."[2]

Heart

Elyse taught me this midrash from Kohelet Rabbah: "I have spoken with my heart." The heart sees, as it is stated: "My heart has seen much." The heart hears, as it is stated; "Give your servant an understanding [*shome·a*] heart" (I Kings 3:9). The heart speaks, as it is stated: "I have spoken with my heart." The heart stands, as it is stated: "Will your heart endure?" (Ezekiel 22:14). The heart rejoices, as it is stated: "Therefore, my heart rejoices" (Psalms 16:9). The heart cries out, as it is stated: Their heart cried out to the Lord" (Lamentations 2:18). The heart is consoled, as it is stated: "Speak to the heart of Jerusalem" (Isaiah 40:2). The heart grieves, as it is stated: "Your heart shall not be grieved" (Deuteronomy 15:10).[3]

We pray several times a day, "You shall love the Creator your God with all your heart, with all your soul and with all your might."[4] We work on attuning our hearts to the Holy Being as a spiritual exercise. If we can love our Creator, then perhaps we can find it in our hearts to love even those who are created in the image of God, but not in our image. Practicing attuning the muscle of the heart may help us in these days to bridge the terrible conflicts which rage between us. We remind ourselves

---

2. Isaiah 40:11
3. Kohelet Rabbah 1:16
4. Deuteronomy 6:5

that everyone has a big and hurting heart, whatever words or beliefs divide us.

Inspiration from Embodied Divine Emanation

We may access our inner divine world by connecting to the emanations of godliness in our bodies. The Tree of Life diagrams of the Kabbalistic *s'firot* represent body parts as well as characteristics of the divine emanations. The central line of *Keter* (crown), *Tiferet* (compassion), *Yesod* (foundation) and *Malkhut* (regal presence) represents the metaphoric spine spanning the from the heavens to the earth and back again. In Kabbalistic thought, *Keter* is a connection beyond thought, beyond creation. We are like a tree with roots in the heavens, with the Divine Creator seeking us. The erotic joining, the pouring of the upper spheres of Divine abundance into the lower spheres are vehicles for the emanation of godliness.

Embodied *Tiferet*, the torso and its beating heart, represent balanced love and connection, compassion and splendor. The Divine abundance pours into *Yesod*, representing the male organs of reproductions, creativity. The *Shekhinah* Herself is represented in *Malkhut*, the female organs of reproduction, or connection to Mother Earth of action. Here our lips and expression lead to prayer and praise. As is written in the *Nishmat Kol Ḥai* prayer, "If our mouth were as full of song as the sea, and our tongue with singing like the multitude of its waves." The lips of our vagina, creation, and the lips of our mouths, enable our lips to speak our gratitude for creation, for being and Being in this world.

This may give comfort as we face transitions such as retirement; we have a changing role in the world, just as our bodies are changing. Our great challenge and goal is, in fact, to function more in the balanced world of Being rather than Doing. Less ego from the outside, and more receiving of divine love, self-love from the inside. It can be a transition of falling in love with ourselves after a lifetime of other-oriented giving and action. What is the divine inside our bodies? The need to praise, to sing, to pray, to dance, to hug, to love, which is the flow from the earth to heaven, or from the soles of the feet where we are grounded, to utter praise, connecting by praying to the Divine.

In deep friendship we can remind each other that we are of value and do not have to proof ourselves by continual action. We can rescue each other in the vicissitudes of life. Some of the indescribable divine wisdom has seeped and trickled down in a lifetime of teaching, learning, and supporting. While we do not have to prove it, we have to love it.

The Second Paragraph of the Shema in the Era of Climate Change

Judith Plaskow, Ph.D.

THE SECOND paragraph of the Shema is a part of the daily liturgy that many people find deeply problematic. Taken from Deuteronomy chapter 11 (vv. 13–21), it perfectly encapsulates the reward and punishment theology of that book of the Torah. As the Israelites are about to enter the promised land, Moses instructs them that if they obey God's commandments and serve God with all their hearts, the land will flourish, but if they turn to other gods, the earth will not yield its produce, and they will ultimately disappear. This theology immediately raises the most serious obstacle to belief in the biblical God: the classical problem of evil. As the Book of Job made clear millennia ago, there is no obvious correlation between people's behavior and their lot in life, whether that behavior is understood on the individual or — as in this case — the communal level. The rabbis themselves sought alternatives to the doctrine of reward and punishment after the destruction of the second Temple, and the theology certainly has not worn well in the decades since. How is it possible to say these words with any conviction? How can they not stick in the throat?

From a feminist perspective, the passage is problematic for additional reasons. It assumes a distant, all-controlling, easily-angered God — precisely the understanding that feminists have been criticizing for the last fifty years. This view of God coheres well with a hierarchical model of society and human relationships, but it is not clear why such a God is worthy of *worship* or how this idea can be spiritually meaningful or sustaining. Most feminist thinkers have rejected the traditional picture, instead seeing God as immanent in the world. They have imagined a God who is present in and through the incredible abundance and diversity of creation rather than a judge who manipulates it from outside.

Already in the 1980s, the Havurat Shalom Siddur project addressed the gap between a feminist understanding and the theology of Deuteronomy, offering a beautiful meditation on the Shema that recast the second paragraph in more immanentist terms. Keeping the original's emphasis on the profound consequences of human action, it depicted these consequences as flowing organically from the nature of particular choices, rather than as being imposed by a superintending deity. The reworking also evoked the beauty and fragility of the world in rich, poetic, and specific language that accentuated the impact of human decision-making.

> Israel, your covenant with God is made of choices: holiness or
> profanity, life or its destruction; you can never keep from
> choosing. If you set yourself to love God with everything you
> have...God's gifts will be yours: a vital earth, its seas and
> continents moving slowly in their own way, the rain and sun and

snow and clouds forming and changing, each in their own way....But if you forget God and choose instead to fashion gods of your own; if they spring up everywhere for you in your endless thirst for something undiscovered, you may lose everything you have....

This was my first encounter with a piece of creative liturgy that made sense of the second paragraph of the Shema, and I carried it my tallit bag for many years. I still find it lovely and deeply meaningful and often share it with people who find the Shema difficult.

But there is also a way in which the impact of anthropogenic climate change has revivified for me the original words of the Shema. I cannot read the second paragraph each week without a tingling sensation that makes me feel that I am hearing not an injunction and a threat but a simple *description* of our current reality. The wealthy countries of the West have for generations treated the earth — and marginalized peoples — as nothing but resources awaiting extraction and use; they have greedily refused any limits and have shown an unwillingness — despite all evidence — to turn away from oil and other carbon-producing sources of energy. Even as they are joined by less affluent nations racing to imitate them, the earth has risen up and is fighting back. In some places, as the Shema would have it, the skies are closed and there is no rain, while in others, the rain comes in torrents that wash away everything, devastate crops, and leave soil moldy and uncultivable for years. Intense heat and unworldly fires kill people, plants, and animals, altering ecosystems that were relatively stable for centuries and threatening the earth's capacity to continue to provide enough food. Human avarice has rendered numerous species extinct, acidified the oceans, and left more and more parts of the world without sufficient water, the basis of all life. There is a real question whether human beings will disappear from the land — not just the Promised Land referenced by the Shema but the earth, our only home.

In this situation, how do we think about the assurance in the first part of the second paragraph, that, if we obey the commandments, rain will come in its due season and the fields will yield ample grain and oil? Might it be helpful to fuse the original language of the Shema with the Havurat Shalom siddur's more immanent interpretation, asking how we can come to "eat and be satisfied," rather than pursuing a path of endless consumption? Certainly, fear of the consequences of our current behavior may be one of factors that leads to a reorientation of our lives, but for change to be real and lasting, it must come from a new understanding of our place in a larger world. We have to make a radical shift, to see ourselves as one species in a dynamic, ever-changing biosphere, to recognize the face of God in the teeming diversity and intricacy of the beings and processes that shape the cosmos. More than we yearn to avoid punishment, we need to recognize ourselves as always face to face with the divinity inseparable from the world.

After One Hundred Seders, a Modest Proposal

Rabbi Sue Levi Elwell

OVER THE YEARS, I have been privileged to attend, and often to lead, over one hundred seders. I have participated in pre-Pesaḥ s'darim, first and second night s'darim, and *ḥol hamo·ed* s'darim; family seders, feminist seders, seders that focused on freedom from drugs and alcohol, freedom from abuse, freedom from traditional Judaism, and interfaith s'darim. We have gathered in sprawling event spaces, glittering hotel ballrooms, functional synagogue auditoria, living and dining rooms — in split-level, ranch, row, and apartment homes on three continents, in college and kibbutz dining halls, in a halfway house for recovering felons, in a federal prison, in a temporary tent during the Covid-19 pandemic.

I was fortunate to spend three years studying the origins, structure, and variations of Passover rituals as I developed a Haggadah to both honor tradition and incorporate linguistic, musical, and artistic innovations.[1] I discovered with delight how, as the Haggadah has evolved over centuries, every telling invites conversation within and between the various parts of

---

1. Sue Levi Elwell, Ed. *The Open Door: A Passover Haggadah*. NY: CCAR Press, 2002

the narrative, even as each participant is invited to see themselves as an actor in the biblical story of slavery and liberation.

Some seders take us on a journey of song, study, conversation, and discussion that lasts hours and nourishes body, mind, and spirit. Some guide us on a brief, compact engagement with our ancient, ever-relevant story. This essay proposes that three brief portions of the seder can serve as a succinct and unique compact seder experience. Taken together, these three portions of the seder, two enshrined in tradition and one the gift of modernity, honor both the Biblical story at the core of the ritual and the rabbinic structure of the Haggadah, while framing the celebration with song and symbol. I invite you to consider whether these three portions might serve, for you, as opportunity for a brief, yet rich seder experience.

Sheheḥeyanu

This prayer, thanking God for giving us life, sustaining us, and enabling us to reach this time, is recited when we perform any ritual act for the first time in a year. On Passover, we recite it after the first blessing: for some, kindling the festival lights; for others, as part of the festival *Kiddush*. One who recites this prayer with intention and presence acknowledges both the precariousness and the blessing of existence. This blessing welcomes each celebrant into a practice of praise and thanksgiving, connecting each individual with every other soul across the globe gathered to celebrate this season. The words of this prayer ground us in time, reminding us that we live in both secular and sacred time, measuring time by the cycles of the sun and the moon, counting the days of our own lives and this time in history. In some ways, saying these words aloud may be a moment of Dayeinu: to be fully present is all that the Holy One asks of us. This may be the only blessing some individuals need to fulfil the seder's challenge: In every generation we must see ourselves as if we, ourselves, came out of Egypt.[2]

Cup of Miriam

Passover 1992 seems to have been the holiday season when a cup of water dedicated to Miriam first appeared on seder tables across the country.[3] Dedicating a cup of water to Miriam mirrors and foreshadows two distinguishing parts of the seder ritual: the four prescribed cups of wine and the fifth cup for

---

2. See also: https://www.myjewishlearning.com/article/the-origin-of-the-shehechiyanu-blessing/, https://www.sefaria.org/Shulchan_Arukh,_Orach_Chayim.473.1?ven=Sefaria_Community_Translation&lang=bi. See also https://www.sefaria.org/Eruvin.40b.11?lang=bi

3. https://jwa.org/encyclopedia/article/festivals-and-holy-days#pid-13325; https://jwa.org/feminism/cohen-tamara-2; The Los Angeles Jewish Feminist Center, established in 1991, included a Cup of Miriam in our 1992/5752 Haggadah. https://jwa.org/feminism/elwell-sue-levi

Rabbi Susan Schnur's "The Cult of Miriam" appeared in the Spring 1992 issue of Lilith Magazine, including a new seder ritual created by three Boston-area feminists. https://lilith.org/articles/the-cult-of-miriam/

the prophet Elijah.[4] As wine is integral to the seder ritual, so is water.

> In the Talmud, the term 'wine' for human consumption and in particular, wine used in religious ceremonies, never refers to pure wine but always to wine mixed with water. The Hebrew expression, מוזג (*mozeg*) usually translated as 'to pour wine,' really means 'to mix (with water).'[5]

Introducing a cup of water in memory of Miriam balances the cup of Elijah that is lifted up near the end of the seder. Miriam, whose intervention enabled Moses to be nurtured by his own parents, anticipates the promise of the later prophet, Elijah, who "brings the hearts of the parents to the children and the hearts of the children to their parents." (Malachi 3:23-4). Miriam, along with Aaron, partnered with Moses in realizing the Exodus; both Miriam and Moses partnered with God in the people's deliverance. Introducing the prophet Miriam early in the seder sets the stage for the essential engagement of children in the ritual, inviting their questions and participation. When water from Miriam's cup is poured into every cup at the table, each participant, including children and

---

4. The biblical figure of Miriam, whose name may be connected to water, insured Moses' rescue from a watery grave and arranged for Yocheved to serve as the nurse for her own son (Exodus 2:7,8), led women celebrating freedom at the shores of the sea (Exodus 15:20,21), and was the source of finding springs to allay the Israelites' thirst as they wandered in the desert (Numbers 20:2). Miriam is the first individual to be called prophet (הנביאה) in the Torah (Exodus 15:20).

5. Heinrich Guggenheimer, *The Scholar's Haggadah*. Northvale, NJ: Jason Aronson, 1998, p. 211

those who do not drink wine, is symbolically nourished by her leadership and vision, just as the wandering Israelites were sustained by Miriam's well.

Ha Laḥma Anya

This brief Aramaic paragraph begins the Maggid section, the central "telling" of the Passover story. In five succinct sentences, the recitation introduces the "bread of affliction," or "poor bread," a central and essential symbol of the seder and of Passover observance. "Let all who are hungry come and eat. Let all who are in need come and observe Pesaḥ." For many, these two sentences universalize the ritual: our gathering is not for Jews only; the message of freedom is universal.[6] The next sentence foreshadows the final sentence of the seder, לשנה הבאה בירושלים (L'shanah haba·ah biYrushalayim), next year in Jerusalem: "This year here, next year in the Land of Israel." The final sentence serves as the capstone and the aspirational goal of the entire ritual enterprise: "Now enslaved, next year free." This brief paragraph tells the entire Passover story, including the challenge to all who are present to become advocates and champions of every individual, across the globe who is not yet free. These five sentences link the past to the present and to the future, completing and complementing the initial Sheheḥeyanu

---

6. We are invigorated and challenged by continuing conversations about the particularity and the universality of the Exodus story and the Passover seder. See Shai Held, "The Power of Passover in Brutal Times." New York Times, 4/21/24, p.10.

blessing. All celebrants who acknowledge the gift of presence listen to the ancient story of courage and faith, and are invited to embrace the responsibilities of working towards the freedom of all who are enslaved.

Each of these three texts unlocks an essential aspect of our precious and beloved story. Each one can be chanted and sung. Taken together, these three texts lift up the sacred calendar and our place in that calendar, the power and rewards of gratitude, partnership between humans and between humans and God, and the dance between the particular and the universal that is a source of the dynamic and fruitful tension that powers all contemporary Jewish study. For those who choose a brief, yet powerful opportunity for study and practice, consider these three texts for your next Passover seder.

The Changing Map of Our Lives as We Live Ever Longer

Rabbi Laura Geller

THE MAP OF OUR LIVES is changing. It is different from the famous map in the Mishnah:

> At five, [one is ready for] study of Torah, at ten Mishnah; at thirteen, subject to the commandments; at fifteen, [ready to study] Talmud; at eighteen, marriage; at twenty; career; at thirty, the peak of strength; at forty, wisdom; at fifty, able to give counsel; sixty is for old age; seventy is for the fullness of age; at eighty, courage; at ninety, a bent body; at one hundred, [one is] as good as dead and gone completely out of the world.
> *Pirkei Avot 1:2*

Whose life is that? Not the life of women in the second century — our women ancestors are not reflected here... and this is also not the life of contemporary people, men or women. But it is still interesting. The Mishnah describes four stages of life. The first is all about learning; the second about building career and family, the third about wisdom and giving back, and the fourth about letting go.

When I was a little girl, if I even thought about it, my map was primary school, high school, college, graduate school, marriage, kids, friends, a dog, community service, and retirement around sixty-five. That's what I saw around me in families like mine where mothers had careers. What came after retirement?

Old age.

I remember how old my grandparents seemed to me when I was young...and they were not even sixty-five at the time! Sixty-five used to be old in the time of the Mishnah...and of my grandparents. But when is someone actually old? One famous answer, attributed to financier and presidential advisor Bernard Baruch is: "Old Age is ten years older than however old I am."

I think about a wonderful scene in the movie Barbie; Barbie is sitting on a bench in the "real world' next to an older woman. Barbie turns to look at the woman and says: "You're beautiful." The woman responds, "I know." Would that in our world one could be seen as old...and beautiful. Or that being old would be in and of itself perceived as beautiful.

The Mishnah says: at one hundred [one is] as good as dead. Yet in the first world, one hundred-year lives will be common for those born today. But, as psychologist Dr. Laura Carstensen writes: "the social institutions, norms and policies that await these future centenarians evolved when lives were only half as long...we are experiencing one of the most profound transformations of the human experience and we need to imagine equally momentous and creative changes in the way we lead these one hundred year lives, at every stage."[1]

Carstensen suggests we need to create a new map of life. We need new ways to think about life after retirement, whenever that might happen. How would institutions and policy change as we imagine that new map and what it means to grow older? Would housing models include more opportunities for intergenerational living, whether in shared housing or in age-integrated buildings? How would workplaces change as younger and older colleagues work together, each bringing their own skills and wisdom to their shared projects? Might there be internships for people who have retired from a career and are reimagining a new vocational or avocational focus? What if retirement planning included not just financial planning but also purpose planning, challenging each of us at every stage to find our *ikigay*, a Japanese term for the purpose for which we wake up in the morning?

What if our Jewish community imagined an intergenerational community not only as "*l'dor vador*," with wisdom flowing from the older generation to the

---

1. From https://longevity.stanford.edu/the-new-map-of-life-initiative/

younger, but "*Dor* im *dor*," generations *with* generations, understanding that each generation has something to learn and something to teach. This is a particular challenge at this moment because we in North America are living in the most age-segregated society in history and yet, for the first time in history, six generations are alive at the same time. Our congregations and Jewish communities are unique third spaces, (contexts outside of homes or workplaces), that can attract both younger and older people. What if we found new and creative ways to take advantage of this possibility?

Jewish tradition offers us a GPS to navigate the new map. It teaches that the world stands on three things: Torah, *avodah* and *g'milut ḥasadim*. Thinking about a new map of life adds nuance to that teaching. Torah is lifelong learning, with younger and older folks learning together, teaching each other, and sharing their life experience. *Avodah* is the spiritual experiences that connect us to each other and to our sense of the Divine, experiences that are richer when we can share them. *G'milut ḥasadim* are the acts of loving kindness that create community through seeing the face of God in every human being.

The map is changing, not only for those who might live to be one hundred, but for all of us. We are reminded of the moment when the Divine calls to Avram and Sarai to begin a journey without knowing the destination. "*Lekh l'kha* (Go, really go)...to the land that I will show you... And I will bless you...and you will be a blessing'" (Gen. 12:1–2)

Listen to the invitation offered by a new map of life. And trust that you will be a blessing. Enjoy the journey.

Afterword

Rabbi Elyse Goldstein

IN 1968, I was the only girl in my seventh-grade Reform religious school class who chose to have a bat mitzvah instead of a Sweet Sixteen. I never once saw a woman ascend the bimah of my Reform temple except to light the Friday night candles — even the mothers of the bat mitzvah girls sat in the pews while the fathers proudly had an aliyah to the Torah. I will never forget the moment I ascended the bimah, read my portion, and opened my speech. I pushed the prepared text aside — the text which had been written for me by my rabbi — and began to speak extemporaneously. I explained how meaningful and important this day was for me, and then I announced that I wanted to become a rabbi. My family gasped. The cantor broke into tears. And then, the rabbi literally fell off his chair. When he regained his composure, he announced into the microphone on his side of the bimah, "No, no, of course she means she wants to be a rebbetzin." "But no!" I said into the microphone on my side of the bimah, "Let my husband be the rebbetzin, I'm going to be the Rabbi!"

Gales of laughter followed in this cute and true story. But for me, it wasn't funny at all. That announcement would be the beginning of a lifetime of not only explaining and justifying and figuring out what it means to worship and lead in spite of my gender but also as much because of it. I didn't know then what it would mean to break a glass ceiling. I was only thirteen and I wanted to change the world. But my intention was highly personal, totally individual. I never thought that women becoming rabbis would shake the very foundations of Judaism, question every assumption of Jewish life that was based on patriarchal power, or challenge what it meant to be a Jew altogether. I didn't realize then that I was in the middle of a quiet revolution, one that would not remain quiet but would eventually echo onto the pages of our Siddur and Maḥzor and into the board rooms of major Jewish organizations, seminaries, yeshivot and even the Israeli government — all within my lifetime.

We pioneering women rabbis got to challenge the patriarchal language of prayer and invent new rituals that spoke to our experiences as women. We got to lead from the bimah using our own style rather than imitating the male Rabbis we grew up with as role models. We got to learn from female scholars. We got to finally wear what we wanted. We got to teach the Torah of women. We went from being barely tolerated "lady Rabbis" to being exotic women rabbis to being interesting female Rabbis to being movement leading female-identified Rabbis. We celebrated the intersection of our womanhood, our personhood and our feminism, and we also sometimes got to be just plain "rabbis" without the ever-present adjective of our gender.

My colleague Rabbi Joseph Edelheit, upon hearing of my retirement, put forth the idea of this volume. "There simply must be a festschrift — a collection of writings published in honour of a scholar — for you, written by your female colleagues!" I am so grateful to him for making me take the idea seriously. My dearest friend, college roommate and soul-sister Rabbi Dayle Friedman took the idea and formed it into reality. I am grateful beyond words for the time, effort, skill and love she put into creating, editing, and writing the introduction for this festschrift; and for her friendship every day. I have been pushing the boundaries of Jewish feminism for forty years, but I have not done it alone. Each of the authors and artists in this volume has a special place in my heart. They are all visionaries, rabbis and scholars with whom, and from whom, I have learned so much. Their scholarship, art, prose, and teaching in this festschrift honour me more than I can fully express. My husband

Baruch's design talents and technical skill were invaluable in typesetting and formatting this volume.

I have had a blessed, rich, and full Rabbinate, with the tremendous support and love of my husband Baruch Sienna, and our children Noam, Yonah, and Micah and their partners Aaron, Tzvia and Myra. It is everything I hoped for and dreamt of when I was thirteen. May those reading these chapters gain wisdom, strength and insight that will enlarge their own hopes and dreams for the future of Judaism.

Contributors

Rabbi Rebecca L. Dubowe is the spiritual leader of Moses Montefiore Congregation in Bloomington, IL. She speaks, writes, and teaches widely on the importance of inclusion within the Jewish community. The greater Jewish Deaf Community has a special place in Rabbi Dubowe's life as she is the first female Deaf rabbi ordained in the world.

Rabbi Judith Edelman-Green made aliyah to Israel in 1984. She was ordained at Hebrew Union College in Jerusalem in 2009; she serves the Reform Congregation in Mumbai, India and as a Spiritual Caregiver at Tel HaShomer Hospital.

Rabbi Sue Levi Elwell, PhD, has enjoyed a rich and varied rabbinic career as a congregational rabbi, congregational consultant, teacher and spiritual director, and editor. A joyful savta, she makes her home in Tel Aviv and Philadelphia.

Rabbi Dayle A. Friedman (editor), is a pioneering leader in the fields of spirituality and aging, pastoral care, and Jewish healing. Her publications include *Jewish Pastoral Care* (editor) and *Jewish Wisdom for Growing Older.* http://www.growingolder.net/

Rabbi Laura Geller, Rabbi Emerita of Temple Emanuel of Beverly Hills, was the third woman in the Reform Movement to become a rabbi. She was a cofounder of ChaiVillageLA. *Getting Good at Getting Older,* co-authored by Rabbi Geller and her husband Richard Siegel (z'l), was a National Jewish Book Award Finalist.

Rabbi Tina Grimberg is Senior Rabbi of Congregation Darchei Noam in Toronto, Canada; her special interests include Torah through Art, refugee issues, and interfaith relations. Rabbi Grimberg emigrated to the U.S. from Kiev, Ukraine at the age of sixteen; before becoming a rabbi, she was a family therapist with a focus on women's issues and domestic violence.

Rabbi Tzvia Jasper is the Assistant Rabbi and Director of Engagement at Temple Israel in Tulsa, Oklahoma, and daughter-in-law to Rabbi Elyse Goldstein. Her rabbinic practice is focused on creativity and innovation, as she strives to make Judaism accessible to all Jews.

Rabbi Naamah Kelman has recently retired from the position of Dean at the Hebrew Union College, Jerusalem. Since making aliyah in 1976, she has promoted Jewish pluralism, Reform Judaism and feminism. She was the first woman ordained in Israel in 1992.

Rabbi Devorah Lynn served as the Para-Rabbi of the Jewish Community of Bermuda for a dozen years and was ordained at HUC-JIR. After twenty-five years of pulpit and chaplaincy work, she co-founded, with Dr. Mirele Goldsmith, JewishEarthAlliance.org, a national Jewish network calling on Congress to act on climate change.

Rebeca Orantes is an international student at HUC-JIR in Los Angeles, California. Her parents are the founders of the first Reform Jewish community in Guatemala, known today as Adat Israel. She has served as a delegate at the World Zionist Congress and is currently a member of the Zionist General Council (Va'ad Hapoel).

Judith Plaskow, PhD, is a Jewish feminist theologian and the author of many books and articles, including *Goddess and God in the World: Conversations in Embodied Theology* (with Carol P. Christ).

Rabbi Sally J. Priesand, North America's first female rabbi, is Rabbi Emerita of Monmouth Reform Temple in Tinton Falls, NJ.

Rabbi Geela Rayzel Raphael is an "unorthodox," visionary rabbi called to art, adventure, and the transformation of Judaism. She is an award-winning singer/songwriter and author of two children's books. For more information on her projects, see www.Shechinah.com.